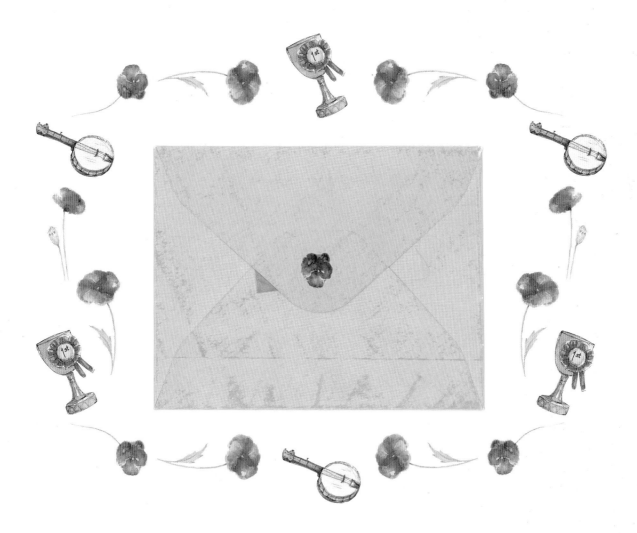

Honeypot Hill

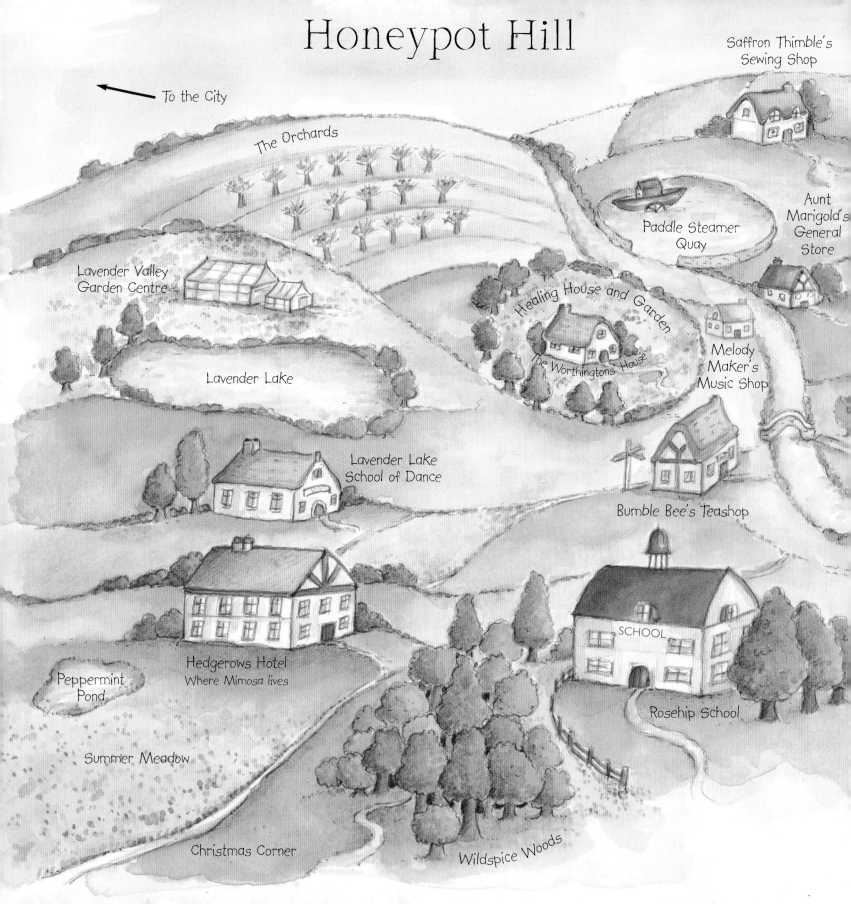

To the City

Saffron Thimble's Sewing Shop

The Orchards

Paddle Steamer Quay

Aunt Marigold's General Store

Lavender Valley Garden Centre

Healing House and Garden

The Worthingtons House

Melody Maker's Music Shop

Lavender Lake

Lavender Lake School of Dance

Bumble Bee's Teashop

SCHOOL

Peppermint Pond

Hedgerows Hotel
Where Mimosa lives

Rosehip School

Summer Meadow

Christmas Corner

Wildspice Woods

Honeysuckle Cottage
Poppy's House

Forget-Me-Not Cottage
Grandpa's House and Office

Poppy Field

N
W
S
E

Cornsilk Castle
and Courtyard

Honeypot Cottage
Honey and Granny Bumble's House

Blossom
Bakehouse

Village Hall

Sage's
Vet Surgery

Re-Bloom
Boutique

Post Office

Beehive
Beauty Salon

River Swan

Barley Farm
The Meadowsweets' House

Riverside
Stables

Honeypot Hill
Railway Station

To Camomile Cove
via Periwinkle Lane

Visit Princess Poppy for fun, games, puzzles,
activities, downloads and lots more at:

www.princesspoppy.com

LET'S DANCE!
A PICTURE CORGI BOOK 978 0 552 57068 8
Published in Great Britain by Picture Corgi,
an imprint of Random House Children's Publishers UK
A Random House Group Company

This edition published 2014

1 3 5 7 9 10 8 6 4 2

Text copyright © Janey Louise Jones, 2014
Illustrations copyright © Picture Corgi Books, 2014
Illustrations by Veronica Vasylenko
The right of Janey Louise Jones and Veronica Vasylenko to be identified as the author and illustrator of this work has been
asserted in accordance with the Copyright, Designs and Patents Act 1988.

Picture Corgi Books are published by Random House Children's Publishers UK,
61–63 Uxbridge Road, London W5 5SA

www.princesspoppy.com
www.randomhousechildrens.co.uk
www.randomhouse.co.uk

Addresses for companies within The Random House Group Limited can be found at: www.randomhouse.co.uk/offices.htm

THE RANDOM HOUSE GROUP Limited Reg. No. 954009

A CIP catalogue record for this book is available from the British Library.

Printed in China

Princess Poppy

Let's Dance!

Written by Janey Louise Jones

PICTURE CORGI

For Louis, my gorgeous dancing boy
and general hero

★

Let's Dance!

featuring

Honey

★

Jonny

★

Rose

★

Princess Poppy

★

Grandpa

★

Ralph

★

Violet

★

It was only two weeks until the Honeypot Hill Children's Talent Contest. Poppy and Honey were busily preparing their acts and trying on their costumes.

Mum popped her head round the door. "Looks good, girls, but it's time to go out for afternoon tea with Grandpa!" she said.

Poppy and Honey chatted non-stop as they walked through Honeypot Hill towards Bumble Bee's Teashop.

"I'm worried about my act," said Poppy. "What if everybody does disco-dancing?"

Just then, the girls were distracted by a boy they didn't recognize. "Who's that boy?" asked Honey.

"I don't know," said Poppy.

The boy kicked his ball
high into the air . . .

It flew towards Poppy
and Honey . . .

And it landed in a puddle with
a big . . . SPLASH!

Poppy was soaked with muddy water!
"Aaarrgh!" she cried. "Yuck!"

The boy ran towards Poppy. "I'm sorry!" he said.

"This is the first time I've worn this outfit!" said Poppy as she shook the dirty water from her clothes.

"Oh, there's no harm done," said Mum kindly. "It'll wash!"

The boy's family came over to see what was happening.

"Hi," said the boy's mum. "We're the Blooms. I'm Rose. This is my husband Ralph and our daughter Violet. Erm, I think you've already met Jonny! Sorry about that!"

"Oh dear, look at your outfit," said Rose.
"Let me give you a dance dress from our
new shop to make up for it."

"How lovely," said Mum.
"Thank you so much!" said Poppy. "I love it!"

During afternoon tea, Grandpa admired Poppy's new dress.

"I remember your grandmother dancing in a dress like that!" he said.

"Really?" said Poppy. "What kind of dancing?"

"Jive!" said Grandpa. "I've still got some of the rock-'n'-roll tunes she loved. I'll let you and Honey listen to them, if you like!"

"Yippeee, I'd love that!" said Poppy. "We can dance to them!"

"This is fun," said Poppy as they danced in Grandpa's living room.
"I wish you could dance with me in the talent contest, Grandpa!"
"I wish I could too!" laughed Grandpa. "But I'm far too old!"

The next day, everybody at Rosehip School was talking about the talent contest.

"I'm going to sing!" said Sweetpea.

"I'm going to tell jokes!" said Harry.

"I'm going to do ballroom dancing!" announced Mimosa.

"Is the new boy going to play that banjo-thing?" asked Harry.

Everyone turned to stare at Jonny. His cheeks went bright red.

"Can't wait for that!" laughed Alfie as the bell rang.

Poppy thought that Jonny looked very lonely.

The day of the auditions came round quickly, but as Poppy queued for her turn her worst fears were confirmed.

"Oh no, Honey!" said Poppy. "Look! There are lots of other disco dancers. How is my act going to be special?"

"Don't worry – you'll be great," said Honey, giving Poppy a good-luck hug. "Oh look, it's Jonny's turn!"

Jonny took a seat and began to play a tune called "Blackberry Blossom" on his banjo. Everything started off well.

Jonny looked up at the audience and smiled.

But when he looked back at his fingers, he made one little mistake.

And then he struck another wrong chord.

Jonny's cheeks went pink and his eyes looked panicky.

He took a breath and started from the beginning.

He was thinking too much now and he couldn't remember how to play the tune.

Just keep going! thought Poppy.

But Jonny was too embarrassed.

He gulped awkwardly, stood up and ran off the stage.

"Poor Jonny!" Poppy whispered to Honey. "It must be so hard to be new AND have to perform in a contest!"

Poppy's audition wasn't bad, but she didn't think her act was special enough for the actual contest.

"You were great," she said to Honey, "but I need to think of a different dance for Saturday! There are too many other disco dancers."

As the girls looked for a table, they saw Jonny sitting alone.

"Come on, Honey!" said Poppy. "Let's sit with Jonny today."

Jonny looked surprised. "You, erm, really want to sit with me?" he said.

"Of course," said Poppy.

"You did really well on the banjo at first," said Poppy.

"Thanks, but I know I didn't," said Jonny. "I'm not going to play in the competition."

"But you should!" said Poppy. "It's fun and you won't be so nervous next time!"

The next morning, Poppy and Honey waited outside the Re-Bloom Boutique until Jonny appeared.

"Hi, Jonny. Shall we all walk to school together?" said Poppy.

"OK," said Jonny. "Cool."

Honey looked back over her shoulder at the window display and it gave her an idea.

"How about if you two dance together in the contest on Saturday?" Honey said. "You could jive."

Poppy looked at Jonny.

He shrugged his shoulders. "I don't mind giving it a try," he said.

"Let's see if Grandpa can teach us!" said Poppy, with a grin.

After school, Poppy and Jonny went to Forget-Me-Not Cottage.

They joined hands and followed Grandpa's instructions.

"Firstly, face your partner and bounce. Then face forward and hop!

"Well done, Jonny. You're a natural!" said Grandpa.

"What about me?" said Poppy, as she skipped and hopped.

"You've always been a natural!" laughed Grandpa. "Next, lift your arms in the air, look back at your partner . . .

"Great! Time for a twirl!"

Ooops! Poppy crossed one foot over the other and tripped!
"OUCH!" she cried, as she took a tumble.

Poppy lay in a heap on the floor, rubbing her sore ankle.

"Are you OK?" asked Grandpa.

"I don't know," said Poppy. "My ankle hurts!"

Grandpa examined her ankle. "It looks all right," he said.

Nervously, Poppy got back on her feet. She was afraid to put any weight on the ankle. She took one little hop. Then a step. Then another. She did a little spin.

"It's fine!" she declared.

"Let's dance!"

At last it was the night of the talent contest. Poppy was super-excited as she stood in line with Jonny, talking over their moves.

"Hey, Jonny, where's your banjo?" asked Harry.

"Ignore him!" said Poppy, but Jonny looked sad that the boys didn't seem to like him.

"I'm a bit worried about that last move," Poppy whispered to Grandpa.

"You've practised all week," Grandpa said with a smile. "You'll be great!"

They danced each step perfectly, just as Grandpa had taught them.

Soon it was time for the special move! Everyone cheered as Poppy flung herself backwards into Jonny's arms.

"My dancing princess," said Grandpa, as Mum and Dad smiled proudly.
Best of all, Harry, Alfie and the other boys crowded round Jonny.
"Well done, Jonny!" said Harry.
Jonny beamed from ear to ear.

Poppy couldn't wait to hear who had won. The announcement was due!
"The winners of the Honeypot Hill Talent Contest are . . ."

"Poppy Cotton and Jonny Bloom!" said Madame Angelwing.

"Yay!" cried Poppy. "We did it!"

Jonny punched the air and Poppy ran over to thank Grandpa.

Poppy and Jonny collected their award and they posed with it while Dad took photos.

But then Jonny disappeared. Poppy and Honey were confused. Where had he gone?

Jonny reappeared with his dad and their banjos.

And they played them – perfectly – for the crowd.

"Everybody! Let's dance!" called Jonny.

The whole dance floor filled up with villagers, and Poppy and Honey
danced and twirled together.